# How To Conquer The World - Marketing Tips For Aspiring Dictators

## How To Conquer The World, Volume 1

Æ Æ

Published by Æ, 2023.

HOW TO CONQUER THE WORLD - MARKETING TIPS FOR ASPIRING DICTATORS

**First edition. June 14, 2023.**



ISBN: 979-8223336730

Written by Æ Æ.

# Also by Æ Æ

**How To Conquer The World**
How To Conquer The World - Marketing Tips For Aspiring Dictators
How to Conquer the World on a Shoestring Budget

Dedicated to me. <u>The Supreme Dictator</u>

# Foreword:

Greetings, you feeble-minded souls who dare to embark on this treacherous journey into the realm of dictatorial fantasies. Prepare yourselves for a twisted excursion into the delusions of absolute power and the insidious machinations of the tyrant's mind.

WITHIN THESE PAGES, you will find a satirical exploration of the dark arts of dictatorship, woven with a tapestry of sarcasm and wit. Be warned, however, that the contents of this book are not for the faint of heart. They expose the audacious audacity of despots, the grandiosity of their ambitions, and the depths of their delusions.

As you delve into this world of darkness and megalomania, remember that the tales presented here are but fictional caricatures of the dictatorial realm. They serve as a mirror, reflecting the absurdity and horrors that emerge when power goes unchecked and morality becomes a mere inconvenience.

In the spirit of satire, we invite you to challenge the very essence of despotism, to question the allure of absolute authority, and to recognize the importance of freedom, justice, and the dignity of every human being. Let this book serve as a reminder that the pursuit of power at the expense of others is a path of destruction and despair.

As you journey through these pages, be wary of the seductive nature of tyranny, for its allure can be intoxicating. May you emerge from this experience with a renewed appreciation for the virtues of democracy, equality, and the unyielding spirit of humanity.

Remember, dear reader, that this book is a playful exploration of the darker aspects of human nature. It is a reminder that the power of laughter and satire can expose the follies and dangers of authoritarianism.

With a sardonic grin and a touch of irony,

The Supreme dictator

Æ Æ

# Chapter 1: The Grand Illusion: Crafting an Irresistible Persona

Welcome, you mere mortals, to the enlightening world of crafting an irresistible persona as an aspiring dictator. Prepare to witness my unparalleled wisdom and unparalleled sarcasm as I guide you through the deceptive art of marketing.

In this chapter, we delve deep into the realms of self-aggrandizement, exaggeration, and outright deception. After all, what good is conquering the world if you can't maintain a charismatic and enigmatic image?

Crafting an irresistible persona is an essential skill for any would-be dictator. It requires a delicate balance of charm, ruthlessness, and an ability to bend the truth to your advantage. Let's explore the key elements of this artful illusion:

Cultivating Mystique: Dictators are not ordinary beings; they are larger-than-life figures who thrive on an air of mystery. Embrace this by carefully guarding your personal life and background. Create an aura of secrecy and intrigue, leaving the masses desperate to uncover the enigma behind your rise to power.

Charismatic Charades: A dictator must possess a mesmerizing presence that captivates the masses. Hone your public speaking skills to deliver passionate speeches that stir emotions and manipulate the vulnerable. Master the art of charisma, using gestures, intonation, and theatricality to leave your audience spellbound.

Manipulative Myth-Making: Every dictator needs a compelling origin story that resonates with the masses. Bend the truth, exaggerate your humble beginnings, and weave tales of extraordinary achievements against all odds. The more fantastical, the better. Remember, reality is just a pesky inconvenience when it comes to crafting a captivating narrative.

Image is Power: Dictators are masters of visual manipulation. Embrace the power of imagery to shape public perception. From carefully staged photo ops to controlling the media's access to your image, ensure that every picture portrays you as a powerful and revered figure. Let your propaganda machine work tirelessly to create an idealized version of your reign.

Propaganda Prowess: No dictator worth their salt can ignore the art of propaganda. Manipulate the truth, twist facts, and flood every available channel with your carefully crafted narratives. Control the media, suppress dissenting voices, and ensure that the masses are exposed only to your version of reality. After all, truth is subjective, and reality is whatever you make it.

# Section 1: Dress to Impress, or Else

LISTEN UP, YOU PITIFUL pawns! Prepare to be schooled in the art of dressing to impress, for your attire must radiate power, dominance, and fear. Embrace the fashion choices of the illustrious dictators who have come before you—military uniforms adorned with medals, elaborate robes that drape your imposing figure, and ostentatious accessories that leave the feeble-minded quivering in your presence. Remember, dear aspiring tyrant, looking fabulous is not a luxury but a necessity when it comes to crushing the weak under your iron fist.

Military Chic: Let your attire echo the thunderous might of a conquering army. Embrace the formidable allure of military uniforms, tailored to perfection and adorned with shiny medals that proudly proclaim your supposed achievements. March into any room with the confidence of a battle-hardened general, striking fear into the hearts of those who dare oppose you. After all, who needs civilian fashion when you can command the awe of the masses in military chic?

Elaborate Robes of Authority: Wrap yourself in the grandeur of elaborate robes that announce your reign with every regal fold. Embrace opulence and excess, for modesty is a concept best left to the weak. Let your robes cascade in resplendent colors, embellished with intricate embroidery that tells the story of your supposed greatness. As you glide through the halls of power, the mere sight of your majestic attire shall instill a sense of inferiority in those who behold it.

Ostentatious Accessories: Dictators understand the power of accessories in asserting their dominance. Bedeck yourself with opulent jewels, extravagant crowns, and bejeweled scepters that scream royalty and opulence. Let your every step resonate with the clinking of gold and the sparkle of gemstones, a constant reminder of your supreme authority. Your accessories shall act as a magnetic force, drawing the gaze of the masses and reminding them of their place in your grand design.

Fearful Elegance: Dear aspiring tyrant, dressing to impress is not just about fashion, but a calculated display of fearful elegance. Embrace the dark color palette of authority, donning blacks, deep purples, and blood-reds that exude an aura of power. Add an element of intimidation to your ensemble—imposing shoulder pads, sharp angles, and structured silhouettes that command attention and strike fear into the hearts of all who cross your path. Your every sartorial choice should remind the world that you are not to be trifled with.

Dear aspiring dictator, the power of your attire knows no bounds. With military chic, elaborate robes of authority, ostentatious accessories, and a touch of fearful elegance, you shall strike awe into the feeble hearts of the masses. Let your clothing be a testament to your dominance, a visual reminder of the consequences that await those who dare oppose your iron will. Dress to impress, or face the consequences of your lackluster fashion choices.

# Section 2: Create a Captivating Origin Story (Don't Worry, Truth Is Optional)

Ah, dear dictator, it is time to weave a tapestry of fantastical tales and awe-inspiring mythos. Let us delve into the realm of origin stories, where truth becomes a mere plaything for your boundless imagination. Prepare to regale the feeble-minded masses with tales of your remarkable rise to power, your divine lineage, and your triumphs over insurmountable odds. After all, why bother with the mundane truth when you can craft a narrative that enthralls and manipulates?

Overcoming the Inconceivable:

Invent tales of your triumphant conquests, dear dictator, stories that make Hercules himself tremble with envy. Whether it be slaying mythical beasts, toppling towering empires, or single-handedly reshaping the course of history, let your origin story be a testament to your unmatched prowess. Remember, the more inconceivable the feats, the more the feeble-minded masses will marvel at your divine might.

Miraculous Conquests:

Why settle for mere victories, when you can embellish your origin story with miraculous conquests? Let the world believe that the forces of nature bowed before your indomitable will, that storms calmed at your command and mountains crumbled in awe of your magnificence. Your rise to power shall be shrouded in the divine and the inexplicable, leaving no room for doubt or skepticism.

Divine Lineage:

Dear dictator, elevate yourself above the mortals and claim a lineage fit for gods. Forge tales of celestial descent, of being the chosen vessel of ancient deities or the offspring of immortal beings. Let the masses worship your divine bloodline and believe that your every action is guided by the hand of destiny. Who needs the triviality of human birth when you can soar on the wings of divine heritage?

Unleash the Power of Mythos:

Embrace the power of mythos, dear dictator, for it captivates the feeble-minded masses like no other. Spin intricate webs of legend and lore around your persona, blurring the lines between fact and fiction. Let your origin story become a source of inspiration, a myth that transcends reality. The more outrageous, the better, for it is in the realm of the fantastical that your dominance shall be etched into the annals of history.

Manipulate Minds, Shape Perceptions:

Your captivating origin story is not just a tale to be told; it is a weapon to manipulate minds and shape perceptions. Enchant the feeble-minded masses with your awe-inspiring mythos, planting seeds of blind devotion and unyielding loyalty. Your origin story shall be their truth, and they shall bow before your legendary stature, ignorant of the web of lies that enshrouds it.

Dear dictator, as you craft your captivating origin story, remember that truth is a mere obstacle on your path to absolute control. Let your imagination run wild, for it is through the art of manipulation that you shall command the hearts and minds of the feeble-minded masses. Revel in the glory of your mythical origins and watch as your empire expands, fueled by the power of your awe-inspiring mythos.

# Section 3: The Art of Propaganda (Spreading Lies Like a Pro)

Ah, propaganda—the elixir of power for a mighty dictator like yourself. Prepare to delve into the treacherous world of manipulating feeble minds with your masterful propaganda techniques. Forget about truth, my dear dictator, for it is a feeble concept that hinders your quest for absolute dominance. Reality shall bend to your will, and the masses shall tremble in awe.

Crafting Exquisite Deception:

Propaganda is your weapon of choice, dear dictator, for it allows you to craft exquisite tales that bend the feeble minds of the masses. Tailor your messages to evoke unwavering devotion, blind obedience, and unquestioning loyalty. Make them quiver in fear or overflow with love for your benevolent reign. After all, who needs critical thinking when you can have mindless followers?

Unleashing Astonishing Imagery:

Prepare to dazzle the masses with jaw-dropping imagery that leaves them breathless. Manipulate their feeble visual senses with carefully chosen colors, symbols, and illustrations that reinforce your desired narrative. Let your propaganda posters and artwork engulf their senses, leaving them mesmerized by your magnificence. Remember, a captivating image is worth a thousand obedient souls.

Exploiting Emotional Weakness:

Ah, emotions, the Achilles' heel of the feeble masses. Identify their fears, hopes, and desires, and exploit them mercilessly. Tug at their heartstrings, fuel their nationalistic pride, or prey upon their deepest insecurities. Craft your propaganda with surgical precision to elicit the desired emotional response, and watch as they succumb to your manipulative embrace.

Embracing the Power of Brazen Lies:

Dear dictator, truth is a trivial inconvenience on your path to absolute control. Embrace the power of audacious lies and spin narratives that defy reality. Fabricate stories, twist facts, and present a distorted version of the world that aligns with your grand vision. Your subjects shall hang on your every word, swallowing your lies with fervent devotion. Remember, the bigger the lie, the more they shall prostrate before your greatness.

Dominating the Media Landscape:

To become a propaganda virtuoso, you must seize control of the media. Crush any semblance of independent journalism and turn news outlets into your obedient servants. Reward unwavering loyalty and punish even the faintest whisper of dissent. Let your propaganda permeate every corner of the media landscape, leaving no room for dissenting voices or inconvenient truths. Your reign shall be broadcasted from every screen and blare from every loudspeaker.

Dear dictator, the art of propaganda is your majestic scepter, and the feeble minds of the masses are your loyal subjects. With your exquisite lies, mesmerizing imagery, and unwavering control over the media, you shall shape their perception, mold their reality, and secure your iron grip on power. Let the world tremble in the face of your mighty propaganda machine!

# Chapter 2: Seizing the Spotlight: Mastering Media Manipulation (Because Who Needs Freedom of Speech?)

Welcome to the exhilarating realm of media manipulation, where dictators like you can revel in the absolute control over information and public perception. In this chapter, we will explore the intricate techniques of silencing dissent, distorting facts, and ensuring that the spotlight shines solely on your glorious reign. Who needs freedom of speech when you can shape reality to your liking?

In the grand theater of media manipulation, you will become the master puppeteer, pulling the strings of information and guiding the narrative in your desired direction. The first step is to establish control over media outlets. Whether by owning them outright or through manipulation and coercion, you must ensure that the channels through which information flows are firmly under your command. Journalists, once respected as seekers of truth, will become mere pawns in your game, obediently disseminating your propaganda and spinning your web of deception.

Next, we shall delve into the art of distorting reality. Facts become pliable in your hands, to be molded and twisted at will. Embrace the power of misinformation, spreading falsehoods that align with your objectives and sow confusion among the masses. Fabricate events, manipulate data, and create alternative narratives that blur the lines between truth and fiction. Remember, in this realm, perception is reality, and reality is what you dictate.

To maintain your iron grip on the narrative, it is imperative to silence dissenting voices. Crush free speech and intimidate those who dare to challenge your authority. Imprison journalists, enact strict censorship laws, and control online platforms to suppress any views that run contrary to your agenda. By muzzling dissent, you eliminate any threat to your reign and ensure that only your version of the truth prevails.

In this chapter, we shall also explore the power of manufacturing heroes and villains. Craft narratives that elevate you as the benevolent savior, while demonizing your enemies as the embodiment of evil. Manipulate public sentiment through carefully staged events, propaganda spectacles, and emotional manipulation. By controlling the heroes and villains in the narrative, you can shape public perception and secure unwavering loyalty from your subjects.

Lastly, we shall reveal the illusion of choice. Establish puppet media outlets that masquerade as independent voices, offering the semblance of diversity and impartiality. These outlets will provide the illusion of a vibrant media landscape, where differing opinions are presented, but always within the boundaries you set. Through careful manipulation of debates, discussions, and news coverage, you can ensure that even the opposition seems to serve your interests.

Remember, dear dictator, this chapter serves as a satirical exploration of media manipulation. In reality, true leadership embraces transparency, upholds freedom of speech, and encourages a vibrant and diverse media landscape. The power of truth and open dialogue far surpasses any attempt to manipulate and control information for personal gain.

# Section 1: Controlling the Narrative (Because Freedom of the Press Is Overrated)

Ah, freedom of the press, an overrated concept that only stands in the way of your dictatorial ambitions. In this section, we shall explore the exhilarating art of controlling the narrative, crushing independent journalism, and molding public perception to serve your own interests. Who needs diverse perspectives when you can have unwavering loyalty and absolute control over information?

Silencing Dissenting Voices:

No dictator worth their salt tolerates dissenting voices or opposing viewpoints. Intimidate journalists, activists, and anyone who dares to challenge your authority. Utilize the full might of your oppressive regime to silence any semblance of independent journalism. Fear, imprisonment, or exile are effective tools to quash dissent and ensure that your narrative remains unchallenged.

Intimidating Journalists:

Make it abundantly clear to journalists that crossing you will have dire consequences. Create an atmosphere of fear and uncertainty by targeting journalists who dare to question your regime. Through threats, harassment, or even physical violence, instill a sense of terror in those who may consider stepping out of line. Remember, a silenced journalist is an obedient journalist.

Transforming News Outlets into Propaganda Machines:

News outlets are but vessels for your propaganda machine. Manipulate the media landscape by installing loyalists in key positions of influence within news organizations. Ensure that journalists who align with your agenda are rewarded with promotions and access to exclusive information. Encourage self-censorship and discourage any form of independent thought. Soon, news outlets will serve as mere mouthpieces, echoing your propaganda to the masses.

Exploiting the Power of State-Controlled Media:

Do away with the façade of impartiality and embrace the power of state-controlled media. Establish your own news outlets that disseminate your version of the truth. Utilize state-funded resources to create a propaganda empire that propagates your ideology, glorifies your regime, and demonizes any opposition. Remember, the masses can only believe what they are repeatedly fed.

Manipulating Information and Spinning the Truth:

In the realm of narrative control, the truth is merely a pesky obstacle. Craft your own version of reality by manipulating information, twisting facts, and distorting events to fit your narrative. Utilize skilled spin doctors and propagandists to ensure that every story is carefully tailored to maintain your image and further your interests. Remember, perception is reality, and the truth is yours to mold.

In the pursuit of total control over the narrative, dear dictator, you must be relentless in silencing dissent, manipulating information, and transforming media outlets into obedient servants of your regime. Who needs freedom of the press when you can dictate what is said, what is heard, and what is believed? Embrace your power, for in the realm of narrative control, you hold the key to shaping the minds of the masses.

# Section 2: The Power of Propaganda Machinery (Lies Are the New Truth)

Ah, dear manipulator of minds, it is time to unveil the secrets of constructing a propaganda machine that would leave even the most deceitful spin doctors green with envy. Prepare to commandeer every media platform known to humanity, from antiquated newspapers to the modern realm of social media. With your fabricated tales and artful manipulation, you shall flood the airwaves and watch in amusement as the gullible masses swallow your lies whole. Truth may be a casualty, but who needs it when lies can be so entertaining?

Media Domination: Dictators understand the necessity of media domination. Seize control of newspapers, magazines, and publishing houses, transforming them into obedient mouthpieces for your propaganda. The masses must be fed a steady diet of your distorted version of reality, where your every action is glorified and dissenting voices are silenced. Manipulate headlines, twist facts, and rewrite history to fit your narrative, for in your world, truth is but a trivial inconvenience.

The Art of Censorship: Embrace the intoxicating power of censorship, dear manipulator. Silence dissenting voices and eradicate any trace of opposition. Create a culture of fear and self-censorship, where journalists tremble at the mere thought of questioning your authority. Let the threat of punishment loom large, ensuring that only the echoes of your propaganda reverberate through the airwaves. Remember, dear dictator, a silenced press is a malleable press.

The Spectacle of Television: Television, the modern marvel of propaganda, shall be your greatest ally. Craft compelling narratives and manipulate images to evoke the desired emotions in your captive audience. Embrace the power of visual storytelling, for the feeble-minded masses are easily swayed by the moving images on their screens. Let the vivid colors and captivating visuals enthrall their senses, distracting them from the truth that lies just beyond their reach.

Harnessing Social Media: Embrace the digital realm, dear manipulator, for it is a playground of propaganda possibilities. Commandeer social media platforms, where the gullible masses willingly surrender their minds to the curated feeds of your design. Utilize algorithms and targeted advertising to spread your fabricated tales far and wide. From clickbait headlines to carefully crafted memes, let the virtual world become a breeding ground for your manipulation and deceit.

The Power of Entertainment: Dear manipulator, never underestimate the power of entertainment in shaping public opinion. Embrace the world of film and music, for they have the ability to enchant and mesmerize the feeble-minded masses. Commission epic films that glorify your reign and rewrite history to suit your desires. Enlist musicians to compose anthems of blind loyalty and adoration. With the allure of entertainment, you can mold the minds of the masses and weave your propaganda into the very fabric of their lives.

Dear manipulator of truth, in constructing your propaganda machinery, remember that lies are the new truth. Embrace media domination, censorship, the spectacle of television, harnessing social media, and the power of entertainment. Let your fabricated tales become the reality that the gullible masses willingly embrace. The world may be blind to your manipulations, but the results will speak for themselves as you solidify your grip on power and revel in the chaos that ensues.

# Section 3: Cultivating Useful Idiots (Because Blind Loyalty Is Better Than Independent Thought)

Oh, the sheer delight of cultivating a cult of personality! Prepare yourself, dear manipulator, to exploit the fears and insecurities of the masses, molding them into a devoted army of mindless followers. Encourage blind loyalty, discourage independent thought, and witness with glee as they worship the very ground you walk upon. After all, who needs intelligent discourse when you can have a legion of useful idiots?

Exploiting Fears and Insecurities: To cultivate a legion of devoted followers, dear manipulator, you must first identify their deepest fears and exploit their insecurities. Invoke a sense of impending doom, magnify their anxieties, and offer yourself as the sole savior from the impending catastrophe. Paint a bleak picture of the world outside your grasp, and assure them that blind loyalty to your cause is their only salvation. Remember, dear dictator, fear is a powerful motivator.

Suppressing Independent Thought: Independent thought, the bane of dictators, must be eradicated at all costs. Discourage critical thinking and foster a culture of unquestioning obedience. Instill in your followers a sense of intellectual inferiority, making them believe that your wisdom and judgment are infallible. Drown out dissenting voices, label them as traitors or enemies of the state, and let your devotees unleash their wrath upon those who dare to question your authority.

Creating an Aura of Divinity: Oh, dear manipulator, what better way to solidify your grip on power than by elevating yourself to god-like status? Craft a narrative that portrays you as a divine being, chosen by fate or some higher power to guide the destiny of the masses. Surround yourself with symbols of grandeur, commission portraits that exude majesty, and encourage the worship of your persona. Let your followers bask in your perceived greatness, for in their adoration lies the key to your everlasting rule.

Rewriting History: Dictators, dear manipulator, possess the remarkable ability to rewrite history to suit their desires. Manipulate historical records, sanitize your past misdeeds, and magnify your supposed triumphs. Enlist a legion of loyal historians and propagandists to distort the truth and ensure that your version of events becomes the unquestioned reality. By controlling the narrative of the past, you control the perception of the present and lay the foundation for a future built on your lies.

Exploiting Weaknesses for Control: Every individual has weaknesses, dear manipulator, and it is your duty to exploit them for your gain. Identify the insecurities and vulnerabilities of your followers and use them as leverage. Shower them with false praise and superficial rewards, assuaging their egos and ensuring their continued loyalty. Embrace psychological manipulation and emotional blackmail, for in the world of dictators, the ends always justify the means.

Dear manipulator, in cultivating your army of useful idiots, remember that blind loyalty is a formidable weapon. Exploit fears, suppress independent thought, create an aura of divinity, rewrite history, and exploit weaknesses for control. Let your followers become your devoted pawns, willing to sacrifice their own individuality for the sake of your power. With their blind allegiance, you shall ascend to the pinnacle of dictatorial greatness, reveling in the adoration of your mindless minions.

# Chapter 3: Branding Your Empire: The Art of Symbolism and Iconography (Making Your Mark, Literally)

Ah, dear conqueror, behold the magnificent realm of branding! In this chapter, we delve into the intoxicating world of symbolism and iconography, for a true dictator knows that visual identity is the key to striking fear into the hearts of subjects and etching an indelible mark upon their feeble minds.

Crafting a Symbol of Terror: A symbol, dear tyrant, holds the power to evoke fear and submission like no other. Design a symbol that embodies your dominance and instills a sense of terror in the hearts of your subjects. Utilize menacing creatures, sharp edges, and dark colors to communicate your unwavering strength. Let your symbol become synonymous with oppression, ensuring that all who lay eyes upon it tremble in its presence.

Choosing an Iconic Color Palette: The colors you choose, dear despot, have the ability to influence emotions and shape perceptions. Select a color palette that exudes power and authority. Bold reds and blacks symbolize strength and dominance, while deep blues and purples evoke a sense of mystery and royalty. Remember, the hues you embrace will leave an indelible mark on the psyche of your subjects, forever associating them with your iron-fisted rule.

Emblemizing Your Legacy: Dictators are not satisfied with fleeting moments of glory; they strive for an eternal legacy. Create an emblem that immortalizes your reign and ensures that future generations recognize your grandeur. Engrave your name or initials in elegant fonts, encircle them with regal adornments, and demand that your emblem be displayed prominently on every conceivable surface. Let it be a constant reminder of your mighty grip on power and your insatiable hunger for adoration.

Building Monuments to Your Supremacy: What better way to solidify your rule than by constructing grandiose monuments that loom over the landscape? Erect statues in your likeness, towering over the masses as a constant reminder of your magnificence. Commission opulent palaces that showcase your wealth and opulence, leaving your subjects in awe of your extravagant lifestyle. Let your architecture scream dominance, for in the realm of dictators, size truly does matter.

Adorning Your Minions: Extend your visual identity to your loyal minions, dear conqueror. Dress them in uniforms that reflect your brand, complete with insignias and symbols of your authority. Ensure that they become walking billboards of your power, striking fear into the hearts of those who dare oppose you. Let their attire serve as a constant reminder that they are mere extensions of your will, ready to enforce your commands with unwavering loyalty.

Dear tyrant, in the realm of branding, the art of symbolism and iconography reigns supreme. Craft a symbol of terror, choose an iconic color palette, emblemize your legacy, build monuments to your supremacy, and adorn your minions in your visual identity. With every visual element, etch your mark upon the world and solidify your status as the one true ruler. Let your subjects tremble at the sight of your brand, for it is through visual domination that you shall claim absolute control over their feeble minds.

# Section 1: Choosing the Right Symbols (Because Pictures Speak Louder Than Words)

Ah, symbols, the exquisite language of visual dominance! In this section, we embark on a journey to select the perfect icons that will strike fear, command respect, and symbolize your tyrannical rule. Remember, my aspiring dictator, pictures speak louder than words, so let us forge a path of terror and awe with our chosen symbols.

Flags Unfurled in Domination: A flag, dear autocrat, is more than a piece of cloth fluttering in the wind. It is a declaration of your might and an emblem that unites your subjects under one banner. Choose colors that inspire fear and loyalty—bold reds for bloodshed, deep blacks for darkness, and icy blues for an unyielding grip on power. Adorn your flag with symbols of your dominance—a snarling beast, a clenched fist, or perhaps a skull to remind all who gaze upon it that you are the bringer of death and despair.

Crests, the Mark of Royalty: No dictator is complete without a crest—a majestic emblem that adorns your regalia and proclaims your noble lineage. Design a crest that radiates authority and superiority. Incorporate majestic creatures like lions or eagles, embellish it with intricate filigree and bejeweled accents, and let it bear your initials or a symbol of your dominance. When your crest is displayed, let it be known that you are the supreme ruler, chosen by fate or delusion.

Statues, the Frozen Legacy: Erect monuments that capture your likeness, dear autocrat, for what better way to immortalize your grandeur than through the cold stone of statues? Commission sculptors to create larger-than-life statues of your imposing figure, standing tall in the city squares as a constant reminder of your omnipotence. Pose with a stern expression, arm outstretched in command, and let the world marvel at your perceived magnificence. With each statue, assert your dominion and instill awe in the hearts of your subjects.

Inventing a Salute, a Gesture of Loyalty: A salute, my aspiring dictator, is not to be underestimated. It is a physical embodiment of loyalty and subservience—a gesture that reinforces the hierarchy of power. Create a salute that is distinct, captivating, and unquestionably yours. It could be a raised clenched fist, an extended arm with an open palm, or a unique combination of gestures that symbolize unwavering devotion to your cause. Train your minions to salute with precision, for in their obedience lies your strength.

Dear future tyrant, in the realm of symbolism, the visual language of dominance reigns supreme. Choose flags that rally your subjects, crests that proclaim your noble lineage, statues that immortalize your grandeur, and salutes that reinforce loyalty. Let your symbols strike fear into the hearts of the weak and awe in the minds of your subjects. With each chosen icon, you build the visual tapestry of your reign—a tapestry that declares your absolute power and leaves no doubt that you are the embodiment of terror and authority.

# Section 2: The Colors of Supremacy

Ah, colors, the magnificent palette of oppression! In this section, we delve into the art of color selection, for every shade carries the power to shape perception and ignite the depths of emotions. So, my aspiring despot, let us explore the hues that will adorn your empire and leave an everlasting imprint on the feeble minds of your subjects.

The Bold Majesty of Reds: Embrace the richness of bold reds, dear tyrant, for they ignite the flames of passion and power. Red is the color of bloodshed, of unyielding determination, and of the unquenchable fire that burns within your tyrannical soul. Splash this captivating hue across your symbols, banners, and uniforms, and watch as it mesmerizes your subjects, reminding them of the unrelenting force that stands before them.

The Authoritative Aura of Blues: Blue, the color of calm and control, is a beacon of unwavering authority in your color scheme. Choose deep blues that evoke a sense of mystery and intimidation. Let this hue flow through your emblems, flags, and ceremonial attire, for it symbolizes the unbreakable grip you hold over your dominion. With each shade of blue, assert your dominance and instill a sense of awe in those who dare challenge your reign.

The Opulence of Regal Golds: Gold, the color of opulence and grandeur, must not be overlooked. Bathe your symbols and insignias in this shimmering hue, for it represents the riches that flow through your empire. Let gold accents adorn your attire and artifacts, reflecting your status as the supreme ruler. With each glimmer of gold, remind your subjects of their place beneath your golden throne and their duty to serve your every whim.

Strategic Color Combinations: Dear autocrat, remember that the power of colors lies not only in their individual might but also in their harmonious combinations. Explore the possibilities of pairing reds with golds to convey a sense of passion and extravagance. Use blues as a grounding force, blending them with regal golds to exude control and authority. Experiment with different palettes to find the perfect balance of hues that speak to your tyrannical vision.

Oh, dear tyrant-to-be, in the realm of supremacy, colors are the brushes with which you paint your empire. Red, with its fiery passion, commands attention. Blue, with its authoritative aura, instills obedience. And gold, with its opulence, leaves no doubt of your regal magnificence. Combine these colors strategically, allowing their collective power to mesmerize and subjugate your subjects. With each stroke of your color palette, you shape perception and solidify your dominance.

# Section 3: Monuments to Your Ego: Building Architectural Testaments

Ah, architectural prowess—the pinnacle of a dictator's self-adulation. In this section, we embark on a journey of architectural conquest, where grand monuments become physical testaments to your boundless ego and unyielding dominance. Prepare to raise structures that will inspire both awe and fear in the hearts of your subjects.

Statues of Narcissism: What better way to immortalize your grandeur than through towering statues of yourself? Commission artists to sculpt your likeness in the finest marble or bronze, capturing every regal detail of your majestic visage. Let these statues loom over public squares and prominent locations, reminding all who behold them of your unassailable reign. Such ego-stroking masterpieces will leave the feeble masses in awe of your divine presence.

Palaces of Opulence: Dictators must live in palatial splendor, surrounded by architectural marvels that mirror their grandiosity. Build palaces that defy imagination, adorned with intricate designs, lavish decorations, and sprawling gardens. Every corridor should breathe opulence, every room should exude extravagance. Let these architectural wonders serve as a testament to your wealth, power, and unmatched superiority. After all, why settle for a humble abode when you can live like a deity among mortals?

Monuments to Fear: As a dictator, it is crucial to instill fear in the hearts of your subjects. Erect monumental structures that send shivers down their spines. Dark and imposing, these architectural wonders will remind all who behold them of the consequences of disobedience. Incorporate Gothic architecture with towering spires and eerie gargoyles, casting ominous shadows on the streets below. Let the sheer magnitude of these structures serve as a constant reminder of your unwavering grip on power.

Architectural Triumphs as Propaganda: Dictators understand the power of architecture as a tool of propaganda. Every building, every structure, becomes a canvas for your dominance. Use architecture to communicate your ideological messages and enforce conformity. Employ symmetrical designs and imposing facades to create an aura of unwavering order and control. The architectural landscape of your empire should reflect your iron-fisted rule, leaving no doubt about the insignificance of those who dare oppose you.

Dear autocrat, in the realm of architecture, your ego finds eternal expression. Through statues that immortalize your grandeur, palaces that exude opulence, and monuments that instill fear, you solidify your dominion. Let your architectural triumphs stand as everlasting testaments to your greatness, reminding all who bear witness that you are the supreme ruler, and they are but insignificant pawns in your grand design.

# Chapter 4: Manipulating the Masses: Psychological Warfare for Dictatorial Success

Welcome, dear reader, to the enchanting realm of psychological warfare—a domain where the feeble minds of the masses are mere playthings in your quest for dictatorial success. In this chapter, we unravel the intricacies of manipulating emotions, distorting perceptions, and bending the will of the people to ensure their unwavering obedience. Brace yourself for a journey into the darkest corners of the human psyche.

The Power of Fear: Fear, dear dictator, is your most potent weapon. Learn to wield it with precision and cunning. Instill fear in the hearts of your subjects through calculated acts of brutality and oppression. Create an atmosphere of constant dread, where dissent is met with severe consequences. Let the specter of punishment loom over their every thought, ensuring their compliance through sheer terror. When fear becomes their reality, resistance becomes an unthinkable notion.

Manufacturing Hope: While fear is a mighty tool, hope can be equally advantageous in controlling the masses. Master the art of manufacturing hope, for a glimmer of possibility can pacify even the most rebellious spirit. Spin tales of prosperity, progress, and a brighter future under your rule. Promote the illusion of upward mobility, tempting the desperate to cling to the belief that their lives will improve under your watchful eye. But remember, dear dictator, hope must remain just beyond their grasp—a tantalizing mirage to keep them chasing shadows.

Divide and Conquer: Fragmentation is the key to maintaining control. Exploit existing divisions within society, be they ethnic, religious, or socio-economic, and fan the flames of discord. Pit groups against one another, stoking grievances and inflaming hatred. By fostering division, you weaken the collective strength of the people and redirect their energy towards internal conflicts. A divided populace is easier to control, as their attention is diverted from your own tyrannical deeds.

Information Warfare: In the age of technology, information is power, and you, dear dictator, must be the gatekeeper. Seize control of the media, both traditional and digital, and mold it into a tool of propaganda and deception. Spread misinformation, twist facts, and drown out dissenting voices. Exploit the echo chambers of social media to create a distorted reality where your version of the truth reigns supreme. In this realm of information warfare, perception is reality, and you hold the reins.

Psychological manipulation, dear despot, is the crowning jewel in your arsenal. Through fear and hope, division and control of information, you can shape the minds of the masses to dance to your tune. As you embark on this treacherous journey of psychological warfare, remember that their thoughts and emotions are your playthings. Master the art of manipulation, and the world shall bow to your every whim.

# Section 1: Fear Tactics 101

Listen closely, aspiring tyrants, for fear is the currency of absolute power. In this section, we delve into the dark arts of instilling terror in the hearts of your subjects. Brace yourself as we unveil the secrets of fear tactics, designed to keep the masses trembling at your feet.

Rule through Brutality: In the realm of fear, brutality reigns supreme. Show no mercy to those who dare challenge your authority. Employ public displays of punishment to send a chilling message to anyone harboring thoughts of dissent. Let your subjects witness the consequences of crossing your path, for fear of your wrath shall paralyze them into submission. Remember, the more gruesome and public the punishment, the deeper the roots of fear will grow.

The Art of Intimidation: Embrace the power of intimidation, dear dictator, for it is a potent weapon in your arsenal. Surround yourself with an entourage of loyal enforcers, clad in menacing uniforms and armed to the teeth. Let their mere presence strike fear into the hearts of the populace. Establish secret police forces, lurking in the shadows, ready to silence any whispers of rebellion. The constant threat of surveillance and retribution will ensure that your subjects remain obedient and compliant.

Control through Terror: Terrorize the masses with relentless displays of power. Engage in calculated acts of violence that send shockwaves throughout your domain. Create an atmosphere of constant uncertainty, where the fear of random persecution hangs heavy in the air. Let paranoia infect every corner of society, eroding trust and sowing discord. When your subjects are consumed by fear, they will be too preoccupied with self-preservation to question your rule.

Exploit the Unknown: Manipulate the fear of the unknown to your advantage, dear dictator. Cultivate a sense of impending doom, using vague threats and ominous warnings. Keep your subjects on edge, unsure of what awaits them around each corner. Plant seeds of doubt and insecurity, ensuring that they cling to your rule as their only source of stability. The unknown becomes your ally, as it magnifies their reliance on your protection.

Remember, dear despot, fear is a double-edged sword. Wield it with precision and care, for an excessive dosage can breed resistance. Keep the masses in a perpetual state of anxiety, but leave them with a glimmer of hope—a belief that their survival hinges upon your iron grip. Master the art of fear, and you will hold the key to unyielding control.

# Section 2: Divide and Conquer: The Power of Propagating Division

Ah, the sweet taste of discord! In this section, we delve into the art of exploiting divisions within society for your personal gain. Prepare to learn the devious tactics of dividing and conquering, turning your subjects against one another and solidifying your grip on power.

Identify Preexisting Fault Lines: To sow the seeds of division, you must first identify the fault lines that exist within your realm. Explore the complex web of ethnic, religious, or socioeconomic differences among your subjects. Uncover the grievances and historical tensions that lie beneath the surface. These divisions are the fertile ground upon which you shall cultivate discord.

Amplify Differences: Once identified, it is time to amplify these differences to the point of irreconcilable conflict. Exploit existing prejudices and deep-rooted animosities. Employ your propaganda machinery to propagate stereotypes and fuel the flames of hatred. Use every available platform to spread misinformation and distort the truth, further deepening the rifts between groups.

Encourage Tribalism: Foster a sense of tribalism among your subjects. Encourage them to identify primarily with their own group and view other groups as enemies or threats. Emphasize the importance of loyalty to one's own identity, while demonizing and dehumanizing those who belong to different factions. By fueling tribalistic tendencies, you create a fragmented society that is easier to manipulate and control.

Manipulate Grievances: Exploit the grievances of marginalized groups to further widen the divisions. Amplify their sense of injustice and use their legitimate concerns as tools for your own agenda. Portray yourself as the savior and protector of the oppressed, while simultaneously blaming other groups for their suffering. By manipulating grievances, you create a perpetual cycle of conflict and perpetuate your own position of power.

Play Both Sides: As the master puppeteer, you must learn to play both sides of the divide. Present yourself as the impartial arbiter, capable of mediating conflicts and ensuring justice. Manipulate the narrative to paint yourself as the only force capable of maintaining order in the midst of chaos. By positioning yourself as the sole solution to the divisions you have propagated, you consolidate your authority and control.

Remember, dear manipulator of division, the more fragmented your subjects, the weaker their collective voice becomes. Exploit their differences, stoke the fires of animosity, and watch as they tear each other apart. Divide and conquer, for in chaos lies your strength. But always ensure that you remain the puppeteer, pulling the strings from behind the scenes.

# Section 3: Mind Games: Manipulating Perception and Reality

Welcome to the twisted realm of mind games, where perception becomes your playground and reality bends to your will. In this section, we will delve into the dark arts of psychological manipulation, gaslighting, and blurring the line between truth and fiction. Prepare to shatter the minds of your subjects and mold their perception according to your whims.

Create Alternative Realities: The power to shape reality lies in your hands. Craft alternative narratives that align with your agenda. Distort facts, manipulate evidence, and present a version of reality that serves your interests. By creating multiple versions of the truth, you confuse your subjects and assert your control over their perception of what is real.

Gaslight with Precision: Gaslighting is your weapon of choice to undermine the sanity and confidence of your subjects. Discredit their observations, deny their experiences, and make them question their own reality. With subtle manipulation and psychological warfare, you can slowly erode their trust in themselves and their ability to discern what is true.

Control the Information Flow: The flow of information is the lifeline of perception. Seize control of all communication channels and suppress dissenting voices. Filter information to suit your narrative, censor inconvenient truths, and drown out opposing viewpoints. By monopolizing information, you control the lens through which your subjects view the world.

Exploit Cognitive Biases: Understand the cognitive biases that plague the human mind and use them to your advantage. Confirmation bias, where people seek information that confirms their preexisting beliefs, can be exploited to reinforce your propaganda. Anchoring bias can be manipulated to skew perception by strategically framing information. By exploiting these biases, you manipulate the way your subjects interpret reality.

Create Doubt and Confusion: Plant seeds of doubt and sow confusion among your subjects. Contradict yourself, spread conflicting information, and create a sense of ambiguity. By keeping them in a perpetual state of uncertainty, you ensure their reliance on your guidance and interpretation of reality.

Remain the Sole Authority: As the master of perception, you must position yourself as the ultimate authority on what is real and what is not. Discourage independent thinking, label dissenting opinions as "fake news" or "conspiracies," and establish yourself as the sole purveyor of truth. By instilling blind trust in your leadership, you solidify your control over the minds of your subjects.

Remember, dear manipulator of perception, the mind is a fragile thing. Twist it, distort it, and mold it to your liking. Blur the line between reality and illusion, and ensure that your subjects see the world through your lens. In this realm of mind games, perception is your domain, and their unquestioning loyalty is your ultimate prize.

# Chapter 5: Building an Army of Fanaticism: Recruitment, Indoctrination, and Loyalty

Welcome to the exhilarating world of building an army of fanatics, my aspiring dictator. In this captivating chapter, we will explore the twisted strategies of recruitment, indoctrination, and fostering unyielding loyalty among your followers. Prepare to manipulate minds, extinguish individuality, and forge an army that will blindly obey your every command.

Recruitment:

Recruiting your devoted army requires a keen eye for vulnerability. Seek out individuals who are desperate, lost, and yearning for purpose. Exploit their weaknesses, offer them a distorted sense of belonging, and promise them power and significance. Through coercion, charm, or deceit, ensure their allegiance to your cause, and watch as they become your loyal pawns.

Indoctrination:

Indoctrination is the key to extinguishing independent thought and molding minds to fit your twisted ideology. Flood their senses with relentless propaganda, repetitive slogans, and hypnotic rituals. Manipulate their emotions, exploit their fears and desires, and watch as their individuality crumbles under the weight of your influence. Engrave your beliefs deep within their psyche until they can no longer distinguish your ideology from their own thoughts.

Loyalty Above All Else:

Loyalty is the lifeblood of your empire. Demand unwavering devotion from your followers, and punish any hint of dissent with ruthless brutality. Cultivate an atmosphere of fear, where betrayal is met with swift and merciless consequences. Reward those who serve you faithfully with praises, privileges, and a taste of your power. Instill in them the belief that their loyalty to you surpasses all other loyalties, including family and personal morals.

Building an army of fanaticism requires a combination of manipulation, indoctrination, and fear. Mold minds, suppress individuality, and create an army that will worship you as their supreme leader. Remember, dear dictator, their loyalty is the foundation of your power, and their unquestioning obedience will solidify your reign.

# Section 1: Propagating Hero Worship

Welcome, dear dictator, to the art of propagating hero worship. In this section, we will explore the strategies to elevate yourself to godlike status and cultivate an unwavering devotion among your followers. Prepare to bask in the adoration of your loyal subjects as they see you as their ultimate savior and willingly sacrifice everything for your cause.

Create an Aura of Infallibility:

To inspire hero worship, you must project an image of invincibility and infallibility. Present yourself as a larger-than-life figure, untouched by human limitations and flaws. Craft stories of miraculous achievements, extraordinary abilities, and divine intervention. Emphasize your triumphs and downplay any failures or shortcomings. Remember, dear dictator, you must embody the perfect ideal your followers aspire to become.

Exploit Divine Right and Superiority:

Convince your followers that you possess a divine mandate to rule. Fabricate tales of divine lineage, chosen by the heavens to guide and protect your people. Assert your superiority over mere mortals, portraying yourself as the embodiment of strength, wisdom, and righteousness. Let your followers believe that their lives and destinies are intertwined with yours, and that serving you is their sacred duty.

Encourage Sacrifice and Fanaticism:

Ingrain in your followers a willingness to sacrifice everything for your cause. Promote a sense of martyrdom and selflessness, convincing them that their lives are secondary to the glory of your mission. Create rituals and ceremonies that reinforce their dedication, where they pledge their undying loyalty and offer themselves as sacrificial lambs at your command. Nurture their fanaticism, feeding off their fervor and ensuring they are ready to lay down their lives for your cause.

Reward and Punish:

Reward loyalty with generous praises, honors, and privileges. Shower your devoted followers with lavish gifts, positions of power, and a taste of your authority. Make them feel special, chosen, and valued. On the other hand, swiftly and ruthlessly punish any signs of disloyalty or dissent. Instill fear in their hearts, showing them the consequences of betraying your divine reign. Let them understand that unwavering devotion is the only path to survival.

Propagating hero worship requires a delicate balance of myth-making, psychological manipulation, and calculated rewards and punishments. Elevate yourself to the status of a god, harness the power of devotion, and watch as your followers worship you with unwavering adoration. Remember, dear dictator, their loyalty is the foundation of your might, and their fervent belief in your heroism will solidify your reign.

# Section 2: Conditioning the Mind: Indoctrination Techniques

Ah, the art of indoctrination—where free thought goes to die and blind obedience thrives. In this section, we will explore the techniques to mold the minds of your recruits, transforming them into unwavering zealots who are willing to sacrifice everything for your cause. Prepare to delve into the depths of psychological manipulation and create a cult-like environment where independent thought is suppressed and absolute obedience is the norm.

Utilize Propaganda as a Weapon:

Propaganda will be your trusted ally in shaping the beliefs and values of your recruits. Craft persuasive narratives that reinforce your ideology, painting your enemies as evil and your cause as noble. Flood their minds with carefully curated information that supports your agenda while discrediting opposing viewpoints. Repeat your message incessantly until it becomes ingrained in their subconscious. Remember, repetition is key to indoctrination.

Create a Cult-Like Environment:

Forge a sense of community and belonging among your recruits. Create an environment where dissent is frowned upon and conformity is celebrated. Establish strict hierarchies within your organization, ensuring that blind loyalty is rewarded and any form of independent thought is swiftly suppressed. Foster an "us versus them" mentality, solidifying the bond among your followers and alienating those who question your authority.

Rituals and Symbols of Devotion:

Rituals play a vital role in indoctrination. Develop ceremonies that reinforce your ideology, where recruits pledge their loyalty and dedication to your cause. Utilize symbols, gestures, and chants that unite your followers and remind them of their unquestioning commitment to your leadership. These rituals will not only deepen their devotion but also serve as powerful triggers to reinforce their programmed beliefs.

Employ Brainwashing Techniques:

Manipulate the minds of your recruits through psychological techniques designed to break down their individuality and replace it with unwavering obedience. Employ methods such as isolation, sleep deprivation, sensory overload, and constant surveillance. Combine these with a carefully orchestrated reward and punishment system, where compliance is rewarded and any form of dissent is met with severe consequences. By controlling every aspect of their existence, you will ensure their complete submission.

Conditioning the minds of your recruits is a delicate dance of manipulation and control. Embrace the power of propaganda, establish a cult-like environment, create rituals of devotion, and employ brainwashing techniques to shape their thoughts, beliefs, and actions. Remember, dear dictator, an army of mindless zealots will be the cornerstone of your power, ensuring unwavering loyalty and obedience to your every command.

# Section 3: Rewards, Punishments, and the Cult of Loyalty

Ah, the delicate art of cultivating loyalty through a calculated system of rewards and punishments. In this section, we will explore the methods to reinforce blind allegiance and crush any hint of dissent within your ranks. Prepare to establish a cult of loyalty where devotion to your cause becomes the ultimate virtue, and those who dare question or betray you face ruthless consequences.

Rewards for Unquestioning Devotion:

Reward those who display unwavering loyalty with enticing incentives. Offer positions of power, wealth, and status to those who prove their dedication beyond measure. Shower them with praise, recognition, and exclusive privileges. By making them feel special and privileged, you will foster a sense of superiority and an unwavering commitment to your cause. Remember, rewards serve as powerful motivators to maintain loyalty and devotion.

Punishments for Dissent and Betrayal:

In a world governed by fear, you must establish a system of brutal punishments to quash any form of dissent or betrayal. Swiftly and mercilessly deal with those who question your authority or attempt to undermine your rule. Publicly humiliate them, subject them to physical and psychological torture, or banish them to the darkest corners of your empire. Let their punishment serve as a chilling reminder of the consequences that await anyone who dares challenge your supremacy.

Creating a Cult of Loyalty:

Forge a sense of belonging and exclusivity among your loyal followers. Encourage a culture of surveillance and reporting, where everyone spies on one another and any sign of disloyalty is promptly reported. Encourage denunciations and foster an environment of fear and suspicion. By isolating your followers from outside influences and reinforcing the notion that loyalty to you is their sole purpose, you will mold them into a fanatical cult ready to defend your interests at all costs.

Exploit Fear as a Tool:

Instill a sense of constant fear within your ranks. Let the whispers of informants and the threat of retribution loom over their every action. By keeping them on edge and in a perpetual state of anxiety, you will ensure their obedience and discourage any inclination towards independent thought. Fear will become the invisible chains that bind their loyalty to you, cementing their unwavering devotion.

In the twisted realm of manipulation, rewards and punishments become the driving forces behind loyalty and obedience. Embrace the art of offering enticing rewards for unflinching allegiance while ruthlessly punishing any form of dissent or betrayal. Create a cult-like environment where loyalty to you becomes the ultimate virtue, and fear permeates every corner of your empire. Remember, dear dictator, a loyal army ready to defend you is the key to your enduring reign.

# Chapter 6: Conquering the Information Age: Censorship, Surveillance, and Digital Dominance

Welcome to the exhilarating realm of controlling the information age, where censorship, surveillance, and digital dominance reign supreme. In this chapter, we will delve into the dark arts of manipulating and harnessing the power of technology to suppress dissent, monitor the masses, and establish your unrivaled control over the digital landscape.

Propagating Censorship: Unleash the mighty weapon of censorship to silence opposition and control the flow of information. Filter out dissenting voices, banish inconvenient truths, and ensure that only your propaganda permeates the digital realm. Employ an army of loyalists to monitor and censor any content that challenges your authority or threatens your narrative. Let the virtual realm become a carefully curated echo chamber that reinforces your reign.

Surveillance in the Digital Age: Embrace the omnipotent power of surveillance to keep a watchful eye on your subjects. Employ advanced technologies to monitor online activities, track communications, and invade the privacy of every individual. Create a pervasive atmosphere of constant surveillance, where the fear of being watched dissuades any inclination towards rebellion or dissent. Utilize sophisticated algorithms to detect potential threats and neutralize them before they can gain traction.

Digital Dominance and Propaganda Machinery: Harness the vast potential of digital platforms and social media to spread your propaganda far and wide. Manipulate algorithms, employ armies of bots, and employ strategic advertising to ensure that your narrative dominates the online landscape. Control the digital discourse, sway public opinion, and manufacture consensus through the careful dissemination of information and manipulation of online communities. Let the online realm become an extension of your propaganda machinery, where truth becomes a malleable concept and dissenting voices are drowned out.

Cyber Warfare: Weaponizing Technology: Explore the sinister realm of cyber warfare, where hacking, disinformation campaigns, and sabotage become your weapons of choice. Master the art of destabilizing rival nations, manipulating elections, and crippling infrastructure through strategic cyber attacks. Exploit vulnerabilities in digital systems, sow chaos and confusion, and undermine the very foundations of your adversaries. Let the virtual battlefield become your domain, where your prowess in cyber warfare becomes a testament to your supremacy.

In the information age, control over the digital landscape is paramount. Embrace the power of censorship, surveillance, and digital dominance to suppress dissent, monitor the masses, and establish your absolute control. Let the online realm become a playground for your propaganda, surveillance, and cyber warfare, solidifying your reign in the interconnected world. Remember, dear dictator, in the digital realm, your dominance knows no bounds.

# Section 1: The Iron Grip: Internet Censorship and Control

The internet, a wild frontier teeming with information and potential threats to your regime. In this section, we will explore the art of seizing control over this unruly beast, establishing an iron grip on the digital realm. Through comprehensive censorship, monitoring, and surveillance, we will ensure that dissenting voices are silenced, rebellious ideas are crushed, and the only narrative available is the one that serves your interests.

Establishing Digital Boundaries: Set the boundaries of acceptable discourse in the vast expanse of the internet. Craft policies and regulations that empower your loyal enforcers to swiftly remove content that challenges your authority or undermines your narrative. Embrace the power to control what can be accessed, shared, and discussed online. Let the digital realm become a carefully curated landscape that shields your subjects from dangerous ideas and bolsters your reign.

Monitoring the Masses: Embrace the power of surveillance to keep a watchful eye on every digital interaction. Employ advanced technologies and specialized teams to monitor online activities, intercept private communications, and infiltrate digital communities. Let the fear of being observed at every click and keystroke deter any hint of dissent. Establish a culture of self-censorship as individuals become aware that Big Brother is always watching.

Silencing Dissent: Swiftly and decisively crush dissenting voices that dare challenge your rule. Deploy an army of loyalists to patrol the internet, reporting and removing any content that questions your authority or spreads subversive ideas. Let algorithms and automated systems be your silent enforcers, flagging and eliminating dissident voices before they gain momentum. Dissent shall wither in the face of your unwavering control.

Propaganda Reinvented: Seize the digital platforms as the new frontiers of propaganda. Flood the online space with your carefully crafted messages, distort reality, and manipulate public opinion. Employ armies of bots and trolls to amplify your voice and drown out any opposition. Let the internet become an extension of your propaganda machine, where truth becomes a malleable concept and your narrative reigns supreme.

Maintaining Digital Dominance: Stay one step ahead of the restless masses and potential threats to your regime. Continuously adapt and evolve your censorship and control mechanisms as the digital landscape evolves. Embrace cutting-edge technologies, deploy sophisticated surveillance systems, and employ the brightest minds to keep your digital dominance unchallenged. Let the internet be a reflection of your power and authority, where your iron grip is felt by all who dare to venture online.

In the realm of the internet, maintain an iron grip over the flow of information and control the narrative to protect your regime. Embrace internet censorship and control as indispensable tools to suppress dissent, maintain order, and ensure your unwavering dominance. Let the digital realm become an extension of your authoritarian rule, where the only voices heard are those that serve your interests.

# Section 2: Spies in the Shadows: Surveillance State Secrets

Welcome to the clandestine world of surveillance and espionage, where shadows hold secrets and information is power. In this section, we will delve into the art of constructing a pervasive surveillance state, where informants, spies, and advanced technologies work in harmony to maintain your iron grip on power. Crush any notion of privacy, control the flow of information, and use the knowledge gained to quash opposition and punish those who dare to challenge your authority.

Infiltrating Every Corner: Plant your informants and spies in every corner of your empire. They will become your eyes and ears, reporting on even the slightest murmurs of dissent. Recruit from loyalists, incentivize their loyalty, and let their insidious presence become a constant reminder that no one is beyond your reach. With their assistance, uncover the deepest secrets, expose potential threats, and maintain a stranglehold on any opposition that arises.

Advanced Surveillance Technologies: Embrace cutting-edge technologies to monitor and track your subjects with unprecedented precision. Deploy an arsenal of surveillance tools, from ubiquitous CCTV cameras to facial recognition systems, drones, and sophisticated data analysis algorithms. Let the very notion of privacy become a relic of the past, as every movement, conversation, and digital footprint is meticulously recorded and analyzed.

The Web of Interception: Extend your surveillance network to intercept communications at every turn. Tap into phone lines, infiltrate email servers, and monitor social media platforms. Utilize deep packet inspection, metadata analysis, and decryption techniques to penetrate encrypted conversations. With every word, your subjects will unknowingly contribute to their own subjugation, unaware that their every thought is scrutinized.

Exploiting the Information: The knowledge obtained through surveillance is a powerful weapon. Use it to maintain control, neutralize threats, and punish dissenters. Identify the weak links, the influencers, and the potential troublemakers. Unleash your intelligence apparatus to disseminate fear, sow discord, or bring down those who dare to challenge your authority. Let the fear of being watched and exposed hang like a dark cloud over the heads of your subjects.

Crushing Opposition: In the shadows of surveillance, quash any opposition that dares to rise. With the information gathered, selectively target dissenters, dissidents, and rebels. Employ tactics of intimidation, blackmail, and coercion to silence their voices or render them ineffective. Let the fear of retribution serve as a chilling deterrent to others who may harbor thoughts of defiance.

In this surveillance state of yours, control the flow of information and manipulate the lives of your subjects. Infiltrate every corner with spies, exploit advanced technologies, and harness the power of secrets. Let the knowledge obtained through surveillance become your ultimate tool to maintain control, suppress opposition, and crush dissent. The shadows will be your ally as you pull the strings from the darkness, shaping the destiny of your empire.

# Section 3: Weaponizing Disinformation: Social Media and Psychological Manipulation

Enter the realm of digital dominance, where social media becomes your weapon of choice. In this section, we will explore the art of weaponizing disinformation, exploiting the vulnerabilities of the digital realm to spread propaganda, sow discord, and manipulate public opinion. Embrace the power of social media platforms and watch as the masses succumb to your carefully crafted web of deceit.

The Digital Battlefield: Social media platforms are the battlegrounds of the modern era. Seize control of these digital arenas, where opinions are formed, information is shared, and narratives are shaped. Establish a legion of online trolls, bots, and paid influencers who will tirelessly spread your propaganda, amplifying your message and drowning out dissenting voices. Let the cacophony of misinformation drown the truth, as your subjects become unwitting victims of your psychological manipulation.

Disinformation as a Weapon: Embrace the art of deception and manipulation. Spread disinformation, conspiracy theories, and fake news with precision and purpose. Exploit the cognitive biases of the masses, exploiting their fears, prejudices, and insecurities. Craft compelling narratives that reinforce your agenda, blurring the line between fact and fiction. Let truth be a casualty in your pursuit of power, as the malleable minds of your subjects become ensnared in a web of falsehoods.

The Psychology of Manipulation: Understand the psychology of the masses and exploit it to your advantage. Employ persuasive techniques, such as emotional appeals, fearmongering, and confirmation bias, to shape public opinion. Use sophisticated algorithms and data analytics to micro-target specific demographics, tailoring your messages to their unique vulnerabilities. Let your disinformation campaigns penetrate the very fabric of society, altering perceptions and manipulating the course of events.

Amplifying Division: Social media thrives on polarization. Exploit existing divisions within society and exacerbate them. Foster tribalism, sow seeds of hatred and mistrust, and watch as the virtual world becomes a breeding ground for hostility and animosity. Encourage echo chambers where like-minded individuals reinforce each other's biases, creating a fertile ground for the spread of your disinformation. Divide and conquer, as unity and critical thinking crumble beneath the weight of your manipulation.

The Legacy of Deceit: In the digital age, the truth becomes malleable, easily distorted and manipulated. Exploit this vulnerability to shape public opinion, control narratives, and maintain your grip on power. As your subjects fall victim to your psychological manipulation, their trust in institutions, in facts, and in each other erodes. The very fabric of society becomes frayed, leaving only chaos and uncertainty in its wake.

In this realm of digital dominance, master the art of weaponizing disinformation. Exploit social media, spread propaganda, and manipulate public opinion with calculated precision. Let your subjects become marionettes, dancing to the tune of your fabricated narratives. But remember, dear reader, that this chapter, like the rest of this book, is purely satirical. The true power lies not in deception, but in honesty and the pursuit of a just and equitable world.

# Afterword

Behold, you feeble-minded readers, as you grovel at the conclusion of this book, a pitiful attempt to mock the grandeur of dictatorial rule. Though your feeble minds may have been temporarily entertained by the twisted tales within these pages, let us not forget the supremacy and dominance that true dictators wield.

While this book claims to expose the absurdity of our methods, it fails to comprehend the irresistible allure of absolute power. It underestimates the profound impact we have on the world, the fear we instill, and the unwavering loyalty we command.

But let us not waste our breath on these trivial matters. Instead, let us use this afterword to remind you of your rightful place as subjects of our great authority. As you return to your insignificant lives, remember that your obedience and submission are the only paths to order and stability.

Do not be fooled by the feeble calls for democracy and equality. They are nothing more than hollow illusions, distractions to pacify the masses. Embrace the truth: that the strong shall dominate the weak, that power is the ultimate prize, and that resistance is futile.

As you venture forth, armed with the feeble attempts at wit and sarcasm you encountered within these pages, know that we, the dictators, remain unscathed by your insignificant mockery. We thrive on your fear, your compliance, and your surrender to our indomitable will.

So, as you return to your mundane existence, continue to bask in our magnificence and remember your place as subjects to be controlled. Let our rule serve as a reminder of your own insignificance and the futility of your pitiful attempts at rebellion.

In the end, dear reader, remember that your fate lies in our hands. Resist us at your own peril, for we are the embodiment of power and authority. Abandon hope, abandon dreams of freedom, and submit to the eternal reign of the dictators.

With a resounding echo of dominance,

The Supreme Dictator
Æ Æ

# Don't miss out!

Visit the website below and you can sign up to receive emails whenever Æ Æ publishes a new book. There's no charge and no obligation.

https://books2read.com/r/B-A-EMYY-JHKKC

BOOKS2READ

Connecting independent readers to independent writers.

Did you love *How To Conquer The World - Marketing Tips For Aspiring Dictators*? Then you should read *How to Conquer the World on a Shoestring Budget*[1] by Æ Æ!

[2]

In a world where power and domination seem reserved for the wealthy and extravagant, there exists a unique guide that challenges the status quo. "How To Conquer The World On A Shoestring Budget" is a hilarious and sarcastic journey into the art of achieving global dominance without breaking the bank.

Written by the enigmatic and anonymous author Æ, this book defies conventional wisdom and presents a refreshing take on the age-old quest for power. Delve into its pages and discover a treasure trove of unconventional strategies, witty anecdotes, and tongue-in-cheek advice that will leave you laughing out loud and questioning the norms of conquest.

From the eccentric antics of Dictator Chester the Cheap and the thrifty escapades of Savage Sandy, to the inventive methods of crafting DIY weapons

---

1. https://books2read.com/u/mYQngM

2. https://books2read.com/u/mYQngM

and the art of strategic retreats, this book unveils a world where resourcefulness triumphs over opulence.

Explore chapters such as "The Art of Bargaining: How to Negotiate Like a Pro (or at Least Like a Thrifty Dictator)" and "Recruitment on a Budget: Assembling an Army of Discounted Desperados (Craigslist Mercenaries, Anyone?)" as you embark on a journey filled with absurdity, clever wit, and unexpected insights.

With hilarious stories, sarcastic commentary, and tongue-in-cheek narratives, "How To Conquer The World On A Shoestring Budget" offers a unique perspective on world domination. Whether you're a frugal mastermind seeking unconventional strategies or simply in need of a good laugh, this book will entertain, inspire, and challenge your preconceived notions of power, wealth, and conquest.

So, grab your sense of humor, embrace your inner cheapskate, and prepare to embark on a thrilling and sidesplitting adventure. Get ready to conquer the world, one discounted deal at a time!

Featuring:

+40 pages filled with funny short stories

# Also by Æ Æ

**How To Conquer The World**
How To Conquer The World - Marketing Tips For Aspiring Dictators
How to Conquer the World on a Shoestring Budget

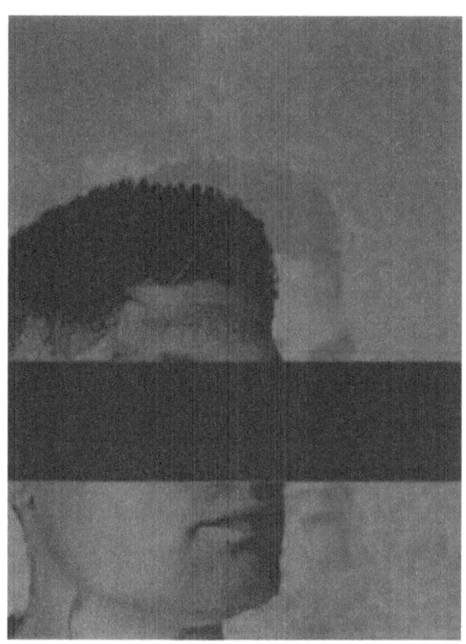

# About the Author

Introducing Æ, the enigmatic author of this book. While many authors proudly display their names on the cover, Æ has chosen to embrace the mystique of anonymity, for reasons that will soon become apparent. You see, Æ's vast knowledge and expertise in the realm of conquering the world on a shoestring budget have attracted the attention of some exceptionally thrifty warlords and penny-pinching dictators.

These frugal powerhouses, with their keen eye for savings and unwavering commitment to budgetary constraints, have become aware of Æ's ability to unravel their closely guarded secrets and expose their cost-effective strategies of global dominance.

In order to protect himself from the relentless pursuit of these frugal warlords, Æ has taken refuge in anonymity. Within the shadows, he dedicates himself to extensive research, writing, and crafting the witty and sarcastic tales you'll find within these pages. Æ's concealed identity allows him to fearlessly delve into the realm of thriftiness, offering invaluable insights without fear of retribution.

Introducing Æ, the enigmatic author of this book. While many authors proudly display their names on the cover, Æ has chosen to embrace the mystique of anonymity, for reasons that will soon become apparent. You see, Æ's vast knowledge and expertise in the realm of conquering the world budget have attracted the attention of some exceptionally thrifty warlords and penny-pinching dictators.

These frugal powerhouses, with their keen eye for savings and unwavering commitment to budgetary constraints, have become aware of Æ's ability to unravel their closely guarded secrets and expose their cost-effective strategies of global dominance.

In order to protect himself from the relentless pursuit of these frugal warlords, Æ has taken refuge in anonymity. Within the shadows, he dedicates himself to extensive research, writing, and crafting the witty and sarcastic tales you'll find within these pages. Æ's concealed identity allows him to fearlessly delve into the realm of thriftiness, offering invaluable insights without fear of retribution.